Lady Luck

A Romantic Comedy
A Deep Heat bonus

By Stacey Broadbent

Published by Stacey Broadbent, Ashburton, NZ
Copyright 2022 © Stacey Broadbent

Originally part of Lucky Star Anthology
This is an extended version.

Licence Notes

Proofreading by Spell Bound
Cover image from Deposit Photos
Cover Design by Stacey Broadbent

ISBN: 978-0-473-62810-9 (paperback)
        978-0-473-62811-6 (kindle)

Lady Luck

A Romantic Comedy
A Deep Heat bonus

By Stacey Broadbent

Contents

Other Books by Stacey Broadbent

Connect with the Author

Dedication

To all the people in the world who believe they are lucky; who make their own luck; or who don't believe in luck at all. This book is for you.

Glossary

Lady Luck is set in New Zealand, so some NZ slang terms have been used. These are not errors, it's just how we speak over here.

Auē	An expression of astonishment To cry, howl, or groan
Kia ora	Greeting, hello
Morena	Good morning
Pounamu	Pounamu is considered a precious and powerful stone by Māori people. It is often carved into a pendant or necklace which carries special meaning for its wearer. Pounamu can represent ancestors, connection with the natural world, or attributes such as strength, prosperity, love, and harmony.

Chapter one

"Did you hear what I said?" I wave a hand in front of Marianne's face.

"Yeah, no I did. I just don't see how this is the massive emergency you said it was. Definitely not worthy of me dragging my butt out of my nice warm bed at seven am on a Saturday morning." She hits me with that look. The one that says I have about ten seconds to explain myself.

"I can see why you would think that, but trust me, it's a big deal."

"I'm going to need a little more than that, Suz. I still had another hour of lazing about with Dallas before I had to get up to meet you." She drags a chair out and plonks herself down, leaning her elbows on the counter.

I huff out an exasperated sigh. "Okay, look. It's like this."

"Hi, Aunt Susan." Toby's croaky morning voice comes from the doorway. He shuffles in, dragging the back of his hand across his eyes as he yawns. "Morning, Mum." He flashes Marianne a smile, and something inside does a little flip. I have never had a want for children of my own, but seeing the growing adoration between these two has had my ovaries doing jigs all over my womb; a constant reminder that the years are moving past at a rate of knots. Hell, as far as I'm concerned, I don't have any baby-making years left in me, but my body sure as shit keeps pushing for it.

"Hot chocolate?" Marianne asks, pushing up from her chair and ruffling his hair.

"Yes please."

"What about you?" She wiggles a cup in the air, and I nod. As if she doesn't already know the answer. If it's full of sugar or salt, I'm in. Always.

"How's it hanging, squirt?" I hold my hand up for a high five, and he obliges, then settles in on the chair beside me. His hair is all mussed up, but his eyes twinkle.

"Ummm, like a…" He taps his finger to his chin. "Christmas decoration?" His brow crinkles as he watches me.

"A Christmas decoration, eh?"

"Mmhmm." He nods emphatically.

"So pretty good then, huh?"

He grins at his mum as she slides a steaming mug of hot chocolate towards him then drags a bowl of whipped cream from the fridge and adds a dollop on top. He swipes a finger through the cream and pops it into his mouth. "Yup."

"Fair enough, kid. I'm pleased for you."

Marianne slides a second cup towards me, holding the bowl of cream up with a questioning brow. "Pfft, you even have to ask?" I watch her scoop a spoonful into my cup, then eye her until she adds a second one.

"Okay, now I'm worried. Two scoops of cream? This must be an emergency."

"I told you it was." I glance at the kid, then back to her, lowering my voice. "I can't get married without them."

"We're talking about underwear, Suz. It's not exactly life or death."

I hold a finger up. "It's not just any old pair though. It's my lucky knickers. How am I supposed to walk down the aisle without them?"

Marianne folds her arms and levels me with a stare. "I knew this was going to happen."

"Knew what was going to happen?"

"This." She waves her hand in my general direction. "You're self-sabotaging."

I lean back in my seat, scoffing. "I am not." She quirks a brow. "I'm not!"

"You're seriously telling me you won't walk down the aisle to marry the man you're head over heels in love with because a pair of knickers has gone missing? Have you checked the laundry hamper?"

I roll my eyes. "Of course I've checked! I've looked everywhere, and the bloody things have vanished!"

"Okay, but why does that mean you can't get married? Go and buy a new pair."

I blink. "Go and buy a new pair? One cannot just *buy* a lucky pair. They're created over time and experiences." I take a hefty swig of hot chocolate, licking the cream from my top lip.

"Do you have any idea how ridiculous this sounds?"

"Of course I do, but it still doesn't change the fact I can't get married next weekend. Without my lucky knickers, our marriage will be doomed."

"You're being dramatic, *Susance*." She pulls out the nickname she uses when I'm being a drama queen, and I suppose it is warranted in this situation, but she doesn't understand. "What's really going on?"

I scrub a hand down my face. "I'm telling you, it's just the knickers. Everything good that has happened to me has been when I was wearing them. If I walk down the aisle without them…" I shake my head.

Marianne reaches out and takes my hand in hers. "You're overthinking this, Suz. Nothing is going to go wrong. Gus loves you and you love him. Knickers or no knickers, you're meant to be together."

"You think so?"

"I know so."

Chapter two

"What do you mean you have no record of my booking?" I stare daggers at the florist who, to her credit, has the decency to look ashamed. She keeps glancing out the back, and her eyes look a little damp. Maybe I'm being too harsh. I take a deep breath and try again. "Can you look one more time? Please? The booking was made months ago. A bridal bouquet and two for my bridesmaids, plus the little doofers that go in the guys' jackets."

"Boutonnière," she says.

"Yeah, three of those."

She clicks the computer, pursing her lips as her eyes dart side to side. Her cheeks flush, and small lines appear on her forehead. "I'm sorry…"

"Jesus, Mary and Joseph." I pinch the bridge of my nose. "Are you telling me there is nothing you can do?"

"I'm sorry." She waves at the screen. "There's nothing here."

"But the wedding is next Saturday!"

Marianne's cool hands wrap around my shoulders, and she drags me away from the counter, leaving the florist with a quivering lip. "Take a breath. I'm sure we can figure something out. I can pop down on the day and pick up some nice bouquets."

I fold my arms across my chest, quirking a brow at her. "It's not the same, and you know it. And what about my deposit?" I swing back around to the counter. "I suppose you have no record of that either?"

"I-I…" She glances out the back again, but whoever she's hoping will come and rescue her, isn't about to be party to my tyrannical rant. "I'm not s-sure."

Marianne steps in, her palm settling on my forearm. "You've kept your receipt, Suz, right?" She turns to the florist. "I'm sure this lovely establishment won't mind giving you a refund, or at the very least, a store credit, right?" She nods her head, and the florist, almost in a trance, finds herself nodding too.

"Umm, yes?"

"Excellent." Marianne claps her hands. "No harm done then."

I pierce her with an incredulous stare, and she simply smiles and nods as if this isn't just the beginning of the disasters in waiting. Goddamn those blasted knickers of mine. How could they up and leave me at a time like this?

I rummage through my bag; the myriad papers and receipts spilling over the edge. There are about ten "free coffee with purchase" dockets and almost double that of fast-food receipts. But nothing with the florist's bright pink logo on it. "You've got to be kidding me." I tip my head back in frustration, searching the ceiling for any help it could offer.

"No receipt?" the florist asks with a touch more enthusiasm than required.

"No. Apparently not."

"Without a receipt, I'm afraid—"

I hold my hand up to stop her. "I'm well aware of what no receipt means," I snap, shoving everything back into my upturned handbag. Turning to Marianne, I point a finger at her chest. "Now do you believe me?"

"It's just a misunderstanding, Suz. A miscommunication. I'm sure it has nothing to do with—" She breaks off and points to my nether regions.

"It has everything to do with it. I told you, this marriage is doomed if I don't find them." My voice cracks, and I cough to clear my throat. This is no time for getting emotional. The very fate of my existence relies on those knickers. Without them, I'll never have great sex again! Oh Lord, Gus probably won't be able to get it up, or worse; I'll dry up like a wrinkled old prune. Now that's a depressing thought.

Marianne tuts. "We still have a week, right? Maybe they'll show up." She places her hands on my shoulders. "But just in case, why don't we head over to see Tui? She's bound to have something to bring you luck until we find them."

I don't see how borrowing someone else's good luck can work, but at this point, I'm willing to try anything.

Chapter three

The bakery is busy as it always is on a Saturday morning. Unlike Marianne, who likes to keep her weekends free to spend time with Dallas and Toby, Tui can always be found out back, covered in flour. When the girls out front told her we were here, she stepped around the counter, dusting herself off and offering a huge grin.

"Morena, ladies." She pulls each of us in for a hug, effectively dousing us in a layer of the white powder too. "Shouldn't you be in your clown get-up?" She eyes Marianne.

"Maid of Honour duties today, I'm afraid. Dallas is taking Toby in my place. He's becoming quite the little character."

Tui chuckles. "I don't doubt that for second. He's got some great role models." She pulls her apron off and ushers us to a recently vacated table. "Can I get you girls a coffee?"

"Please. I think it's needed today." Marianne pulls a face.

"Make mine a double shot. Or better yet, Irish. Maybe more Irish than coffee." I slump into my seat, resting my forehead against the table and instantly regretting it. "There's something sticky on here." I peel my face from the wood and roll my eyes. "Figures."

Marianne stifles a laugh at my expense. I get it. I'd laugh too if it was the other way around. She probably thinks I'm a mental case ready to be admitted to the loony bin. Hell, maybe I should admit myself. It would certainly be better than ruining the only good relationship I've ever had. I'm sure Gus would understand. I'd be doing him a favour.

"Whatever you're thinking, stop it. Everything is going to be fine." Marianne slides her hand across the table then thinks better of it, pulling back before she too ends up with whatever jam/custard concoction is smeared across my forehead.

Tui comes back with our drinks and a damp cloth. She takes care of the table, then offers me a napkin to clean up.

I peer into my mug, inhaling the rich aroma of strong coffee with a hint of something else. Port perhaps? I crinkle my nose, and she chuckles.

"We only had cooking sherry."

"You know what? I don't even care." I take a sip and force it down. One eye flickers of its own volition. "It's fine," I rasp out, pushing the mug across the table.

"Alright, what gives?" Tui folds her arms across her ample chest. "You get married next week. You're meant to be excited, not whatever this is."

"She can't find her lucky knickers, and now she thinks the marriage is doomed."

"Auē, girl. You're moping over a pair of knickers?" Tui leans back in her seat, a throaty laugh falling from her lips. "I've got loads of knickers if you want some, girl. All you had to do was ask." Her shoulders bounce as she laughs again.

"Thanks, but no thanks. I've got plenty of pairs myself, just not the pair I need."

Marianne jumps in. "We were hoping maybe you would have something else she could borrow for a bit of luck." She turns to me with a look of glee. "Ooh, it could be your something borrowed for on the day."

I feign excitement, swirling a finger in the air. "Yay."

"This is really important to you, huh?" Tui wipes a hand across her eyes, leaving a smear of flour across her forehead. "All I can offer you is a pounamu, but I can't loan you one of mine. It has to be gifted to you, and it needs to be blessed."

"That sounds perfect, right, Suz?" Marianne's hopeful grin is infectious, and I find myself smiling back. Maybe this could work.

"It'll take me a few days to find the right piece and have it blessed, but I know some people. Leave it with me."

"Thanks, Tui. I appreciate it. After this morning's flower debacle, I was starting to lose hope."

"Flower debacle?" Tui quirks a brow, and Marianne fills her in on our disastrous morning. "Auē, that's unfortunate. I can see why you'd think you're having bad luck, but, girl, you know every wedding has something go wrong, right? You just have to go with the flow." She waves her hands through the air.

"Easy for you to say. You've been married to the old balls and schlong for a decade."

Tui barks out a laugh, and Marianne's cheeks puff out as she tries to keep her mouthful of coffee from spraying outwards. "You sure do have a way with words. I hope Gus knows what he's getting himself into."

"He's been *getting himself into* me more times than I can count, so yeah, I think he does." I waggle my brows, and Tui shakes her head.

"Girl, you are something else."

Chapter Four

There's an incessant buzzing noise behind my head, and I try to swat it away with a backwards slap of my hand. It continues, and I roll over with a groan. "Okay, okay, keep your panties on." Squinting in the early morning light, I hit the stop button on my phone alarm and toss it on the bed beside me. Whose hare-brained idea was it to book a Sunday morning hair appointment?

There's a chuckle beside me, and I twist my head to meet Gus's gaze. He reaches out and tucks a strand of hair behind my ear, as if that's the only thing out of place first thing in the morning. Judging by the cold breeze on my chest, I'd hazard a guess that one, if not both, nipples have escaped the clutches of my singlet and are hanging loose and free. I guess the girls needed to breathe.

"This time next week you'll be Mrs. Callaghan." He beams, and his eyes don't even hint at turning downwards to my exposed breasts. Any other bloke would be headfirst into a motorboat, but not my Gus. How I managed to snag myself the only remaining gentleman on the face of the planet is beyond me. I'm not exactly the ladylike type, and I'm up for almost anything in the bedroom.

I wasn't even looking, truth be told. He just kind of fell into my lap; and not even face first. It was all a bit weird for me to start with, but his forever hopeful, full-of-positivity way of life kind of grew on me, and he wore me down. I wasn't used to men being so… what's the word? *Nice.*

One and done; that had been my motto for years. Don't get attached and you won't get hurt. I tried to keep him at a distance, but he was persistent. Always sending me lovey-dovey messages that on any normal day would've had my head hanging over the porcelain bowl. But for whatever reason, he kept on reaching out, and I kept on responding. Now three years later, we're about to tie the knot—if I can manage to make it that far without my good luck charm.

"So you haven't changed your mind then?" I snort, twisting the fabric of my singlet until it's back in position.

"Of course I haven't. Have you?" He leans up on one elbow, his eyebrow raised in question.

"No… I was just checking before I go and blow $300 on a new cut and colour for the big day." I sweep the duvet across to his side and swing my legs out of bed. I bunch my hair on top of my head and peer at him over my shoulder. "I'm getting the whole lot cut off and dying my head like a rainbow."

His eyes shine as he plants a kiss to my bare shoulder. "Excellent. I'll go tie shopping and find one to match." He winks, wrapping his arms around my waist. He says it as if he's joking, but I know he'd do it if he thought I wanted him to. I learnt that after casually mentioning how men are getting the old back, sack and crack done these days, and he went straight out and did it the next day. I'm not going to lie, it was nice, but not at all what I had meant for him to do. I happen to like my men with a bit of hair on their bodies. A dusting of stubble, a few curls on their chest, and downstairs should remain as the good Lord created it. I do, however, draw the line at a hairy back. If it looks like you're wearing a sweater when you're not; we have a problem.

"You wouldn't care if I showed up with my hair shaved off?"

"If that's what makes you happy, go for it." He runs a hand across his cropped locks. "I know how much you like to run your hands through my hair."

I can't help but laugh. "Well, yeah, but I'm not really going to shave it. I might cut it shorter though. Maybe a bob?" Jesus, what's happening to me? Since when do I care what anyone thinks?

Since I lost the one thing that could make or break this marriage, that's when.

"Whatever you like. I'm sure you'll look fantastic either way." He kisses my shoulder again before pushing up off the bed and heading for the shower.

Nothing seems to flap him; which is probably a good thing, all things considered. If he'd be happy for me to show up to our wedding with a shaved rainbow head, then really, what do I have to worry about?

Chapter five

"It's purple." My eyebrows have flown to the farthest reaches of my forehead as I gape at my reflection. No matter which way I turn, it looks the same. Bright purple. Like the colour of Grimace.

"Yeah, looks great, right?" The hairdresser grins from behind me, wrapping the cord around the hairdryer.

"Um, that's one word for it."

The hairdresser sets the hairdryer on her workstation, then squirts some product into her hands. She scrunches my curls, and somehow that makes the colour stand out even more than before. I look like some kind of berry. Or worse, like the purple rinse brigade left their colour in too long.

She must notice the horror on my face because she stops scrunching and tilts her head. "You don't like it?"

"I don't remember asking to look like a blackcurrant, that's all." I rip the apron from around my neck and grab my bag.

She frowns. "But you said you wanted it to look purple."

"*Fleur Hill*. I said I want to look like Fleur Hill! You know, the actress from *Eager Beavers*." I punch her name into my phone and hold it out for her to see.

"Oh." She draws the word out then sucks her bottom lip in between her teeth. "My bad."

"Damn right it's your bad! I'm getting married in less than a week, and now I'm going to look like a bloody blueberry!"

"Technically it's more of a boysenb—" I hit her with a stare, and she stops. "Sorry."

With a shake of my head, I tuck my phone back into my purse and stand. "I'm not paying for this."

Her face drops. "But… that was three hours… and we haven't even cut it yet… all that colour…"

I hold a finger up. "Colour I didn't ask for." Closing my eyes, I inhale deeply through my nose. "I'll pay half, for your time. But I think we can both agree this is not what I came in here for. I'm not wasting any more time on a cut that I don't want as well."

"But that'll come out of my wages."

"And I'll look like a beauty school dropout on my wedding day. There's no winner here."

Her brow furrows in confusion, and it's abundantly clear she has no clue what I'm referring to.

"Jesus H. Christ, how old are you?"

"I just turned 21." She grins, and I inwardly cringe. For the first time, I feel every one of my 44 years. No wonder she doesn't understand me. I like to think I'm keeping up with things, but when it comes down to it, we're generations apart. I'm what the youngsters refer to as an elder millennial, while she's generation XYZ or something. This was doomed from the start.

"Wow, that's…" Gus leans back in his chair, his eyes like saucers as he takes in my new colour. "You weren't joking when you said you were going for something different."

"Believe me, this is not what I had in mind." I toss my bag on the floor and flop down on the couch. "It looks like someone spilled Ribena on my head."

He chuckles as he stands. His hands land on my shoulders, and he starts to knead. I moan, sinking further into the couch.

"It's not that bad. I actually kinda like it." He presses a kiss to my forehead, and I glare at him.

"You have to say that."

He shrugs. "Happy wife, happy life."

"Ah, therein lies the problem." I point at the monstrosity on my head. "This does not a happy wife make."

"Oh, come on." He skirts around the couch and sits next to me. "Where's my Queen Suz gone, huh?

The fierce woman I fell in love with who doesn't give a damn what anyone thinks? Hmm?"

I give him a side eye. "It's *Susance*, and she's still here. It's just… this day means more than anything else ever has. It's a big deal. I want it to be perfect for you."

He tilts my chin. "As long as you don't leave me stranded at the altar, it will be perfect. All I need is you."

I make a gagging sound and mime sticking my finger down my throat. He laughs, and I snuggle into him. I can joke about these things, but deep down, when he says all that mushy stuff that used to make me roll my eyes and cringe, it makes my heart flutter and my insides go all squirmy. That's how I know this is the real deal. It's also why I'm so desperate to find my lucky knickers. It's like a snowball effect. First they go missing, then the florist bails on me, and now my head looks like it's holding a bunch of grapes. And there's still five days until we tie the knot. Five more days of disasters.

I hope to God Tui comes through with the pounamu. At least then I'll have some good juju coming my way and I won't have to worry anymore.

Chapter six

With a silk scarf wrapped around my head and a take-no-prisoners attitude, I strut into work Monday morning as if I own the world. Lost knickers, purple hair, and no flowers aside, I have work to do before I take leave for our wedding and honeymoon, and I will not allow that bad luck to stand in my way. Come hell or high water, I *will* be hitting the road with Gus this weekend, and I won't be looking back.

"Thank God you're here."

Oh shit. Don't get me wrong, it's always nice to be needed, but when your office junior comes running at you before your morning coffee, it's never a good sign.

"Somebody better be dead or dying. I've literally just walked through the door. I haven't even set my bag down or made a coffee." I fold my arms across my chest and level her with a stare.

Her shoulders hunch in and she shuffles from foot to foot. "I thought I would get a head start on the wages for you…"

I hold up a hand. "I'm going to stop you right there. Unless that sentence is followed by *everything is all in order and waiting for you to process,* I don't want to hear it."

"Um." She glances over her shoulder. "Okay?"

I pinch the bridge of my nose. "Jesus. H. Christ. What did you do?"

She wrings her fingers together and her bottom lip begins to shake. "I, um, I followed the instructions you printed out…" Her voice is barely more than a whisper.

"You've put them through already?"

She nods, blinking back tears. "I know you have a busy load over the next few days, and I thought I could help, but…" She glances over her shoulder again. "I fucked up." Her head snaps around to face me, and she winces. "I mean, I messed up."

I take a deep breath and snag my seat back, swinging it towards me before sitting down. "Walk me through it."

"I entered all the hours like normal, but when I transferred it to payroll, it somehow changed everything. I tried to edit it, but I accidentally hit authorise instead of edit and—" she points, "—it processed it with the wrong numbers."

Glancing over the printout, it's obvious what's happened. "Who was the last person you put hours in for?"

"Hayley, from line one. She's the new girl."

"I know who she is," I snap, then take another calming breath. "You transferred her hours to everyone, that's why it doesn't match. I'll have to adjust them all manually and make an extra payment."

"Sorry."

I wave her off. "It's fine." *It's not fine.* "Pass me the timesheets and I'll get this fixed up."

She trots to her desk then back again, handing over the wad of papers. "Is there anything I can do to help?" She bites her lip, and I turn a raised brow to her. "Coffee?" she suggests, and it may just be her saving grace at this point.

"Black with four sugars."

"F-four?"

She has the audacity to question *my* numbers? "Yes. Four." I hold up four fingers. "In case you hadn't noticed, I'm far from sweet enough this morning." I huff out a breath as I pull the timesheets towards me and start sorting them out.

The scarf I have wrapped around my hair slowly unwinds and falls unceremoniously in front of my face. "Of course," I seethe through gritted teeth as I pull it from my head and start again.

Fiona gasps from behind me but doesn't say a word as she places my coffee beside me. Her eyes bore into the side of my head.

"Yes, my hair is purple. No, it's not what I asked for. Yes, I'm stuck with it for the wedding." I turn to her, daring her to mock me.

"It's purple? I hadn't even noticed." She smiles cautiously, then turns and heads back to her desk.

All morning, she sneaks glances my way, and anyone who passes does a double take. It would be comical if it weren't for the snickering too.

After the third time retying the scarf, I take a deep breath. What would Miss Bee do?

I pull the blasted thing from my head and throw it in the trashcan where it belongs.

When I trudge my way through to the kitchen at six o'clock, the smell of butter chicken hits my nostrils, and I inhale deeply. Being single had its benefits all those years, but nothing beats coming home from an exhausting day to a homecooked meal that I didn't have to make.

"Honey, I'm home," I sing as I traipse across the floor to drape myself around Gus. My breathing falls in sync with his, and the day from hell slowly dissipates.

He bends to plant a kiss on the tip of my nose, and I crinkle it up as I grin at him. "You're in a better mood than yesterday."

"I am now that I'm home." I unwrap myself from around him and swipe a wine glass down from the shelf, grabbing a bottle from the fridge. I pour a hefty glug into my glass then quickly bring it to my lips. My eyes fall closed as I let out a sigh.

Gus turns away from the stove, folding his arms. "Rough day?"

I blink my eyes open, turning back to the fridge to grab him a beer. "Not rough, but busy. I was putting out fires left, right and bloody centre all day." Cracking open the beer, I hand it to him. "I swear that place will go down the crapper while I'm away next week."

He sets the beer aside then tugs at my blouse, pulling me into his arms. "They're lucky to have you, but they're going to have to figure out how to survive without you, because I'm not giving up our honeymoon." His lips brush mine, and like it always does, a tingle of excitement pulses through me. I push up on my toes to deepen the kiss, moaning when he pulls back with a chuckle. "You need to tell them you won't be reachable. I have plans on keeping you busy the *whole* week." He waggles his brows.

"Damn right you will be, Mr Callaghan. I wanna be walking around here like a goddamn cowboy when we return."

He smirks, and his lips dance closer to mine. "I think that can be arranged."

Chapter seven

"Oh my God, Tui, it's beautiful." I hold the braided green stone in my hands, rubbing my forefinger gently over the curves. "It's perfect. Thank you."

Tui grins, resting her hands across her stomach. "My pleasure, girl. I hope it brings harmony to your big day."

"I need all the help I can get, clearly." I tug the beanie from my hair and let my purple curls fall around my face. My so-called friends manage to hold it together for all of three seconds before they start laughing.

"What did you do?" Marianne picks up a lock of hair, inspecting it. "Was this like that time we got drunk and coated my hair in cooking oil? Did you have too many wines last night?"

"Unfortunately, no. This is three days old now, and I've been washing it twice a day to dull the tone, but the bloody colour is staying strong."

She stifles her laughter with her hand. "So this was on purpose?"

"No it wasn't on purpose! The hairdresser misheard me, and that was the only appointment they had free this week, so I'm stuck with it."

Tui holds up a full bottle of cooking oil with a grin. "You want to try this?"

"Believe me, I have considered it, but no. Saturday is far too important to try an old wives tale. If something goes wrong, I'm screwed." I grimace. "More screwed than I already am. Better the devil you know, right?"

"That's true. I mean, purple hair is one thing, but greasy purple hair is worse." Marianne's eyes widen. "What if we dye it darker?"

"Darker? Do you not remember when I dyed it black years ago?" I cringe, shaking my head. "I looked like death warmed up. No. I think I'm better off leaving it the way it is."

"Even if you *do* look like Violet Beauregarde." Marianne snickers, waving her hands in front of her face. "Sorry. I'm done now." Her lips pull in tight like she's trying to keep in a laugh.

I turn my attention back to the necklace and pull the leather cord over my head, adjusting the length until the pounamu is sitting at the base of my neck. "How does it look?"

"Stunning," Marianne says, and Tui agrees.

"And don't worry about the whole blueberry-on-top-of-a-pav look. It's unique, just like you, girl." Tui places her hand on my shoulder. "If anyone can pull off purple hair on their wedding day, it's you. Just give them a bit of the old Queen Bee attitude." She prances around her kitchen, twisting her hand front and back like the single ladies in the dance video.

"Now *that* I can do." I step in behind her, mimicking her actions. "Ooh! That reminds me, have you two been practicing your walk down the aisle?"

Marianne and Tui exchange a look. "I hate to break it to you, but we've known how to walk for a while now, Suz."

I roll my eyes. "We're not *walking*, we're strutting. *Crazy in Love*, remember?" I fish my phone out of my bag and press play, turning the volume up as high as it will go. The sound of trumpets and drums ring out, and I count out loud. "One, two, three, and…" I take exaggerated steps, swinging my hips as I strut between her kitchen counters to the beat of the music. "And then you come in, Tui." I walk back down to where they're watching me with amused expressions on their faces. "And then it's all me, baby." I make a move like I'm busting through a set of doors then cross each leg in front of the other, pushing my hips out even further. "I want people to think they're going to lose their eyes with all the hip action."

Tui taps her leg. "I don't know if my knee can handle that. That's a whole lot of hip swinging there, girl, and I ain't no spring chicken anymore."

I wave a hand through the air. "That's fine. You won't upstage me then." I wink, and she tosses a tea towel at me.

"Like anyone could upstage you."

"Well—" I flick my hair, "—I do know how to work a room."

"You certainly do. No one will be able to take their eyes off you." Marianne grins. "Especially with that hair."

Chapter eight

I wake to a ring of fire. Rolling onto my back, I wince as a sharp pain bites around the leather cord hanging around my neck. The only spot that doesn't hurt is where the pounamu rests against my skin. Perhaps I shouldn't have slept with it on. Or maybe I should've loosened it first. I run tentative fingers across the base of my neck and find large welts have formed into what I'm sure looks like an unsightly necklace of raw skin. I don't know why I'm surprised really.

I roll out of bed, careful not to disturb Gus on our last morning of living in sin. Today, he's off to stay with his best man, Dylan, while Marianne and Tui come to keep me from going insane. We won't see each other again until I'm walking down the aisle, and I hope to God nothing else goes wrong before then.

I pad through to the bathroom and stop in front of the mirror. It's worse than I thought. Not only are there welts surrounding my neck, there's also a vicious-looking rash running up towards my chin. I ease my fingers between the cord and my skin, slowly loosening it enough to drag over my head. "You've got to be kidding me," I hiss under my breath as I twist and turn in front of my reflection. Without the necklace on, I look as though someone has been strangling me. That's a great look for the wedding day.

I throw open the drawers, rummaging around for something to soothe the burning. Thoughts of leaving Gus to sleep in are long forgotten as I fight back angry tears. This is the sort of thing that happens to Marianne while I sit back and make jokes, not the other way around. I slam the drawer shut and make my way back to the bedroom for my phone. If anyone can help me, it'll be Marianne. She's always getting herself into situations like this, and she *is* married to a doctor. I bet she has all manner of creams I could use.

"Morning," Gus mumbles as he rolls over, his arm reaching across the bed towards me.

"Don't look at me." I grab my dressing gown and throw it over my head as I snatch my phone from the nightstand and shuffle down the hall before he can see the state I'm in. I send a quick S.O.S text to Marianne then sit back on the couch to wait for her reply. When Gus comes out, he looks confused, and I don't blame him. I haven't been myself these past few days. I know I can't keep blaming the missing knickers for this, but I don't know what's gotten into me.

I pull my gown tight around my neck and hunch farther down on the couch, putting my feet up on the coffee table and bobbing my knees up and down.

Gus sits beside me and places his hand on my knee to stop it. The warmth of his hand is calming, and yet it makes me want to cry. I wanted our day to be perfect, but nothing is going right. If I was a religious person, I'd say I was being tested, but that's a load of bullshit. It feels more like I'm being pranked than tested.

"What's going on?" Gus searches my eyes with a frown. He removes his hand from my knee, and I instantly miss the contact. "Are you having second thoughts?"

"No! Of course not." I twist so that my knees fall to his lap, but I keep my hands firmly clasping the gown tight. "I want nothing more than to be your wife, I promise."

"Then what is it?"

"You know how things have been going wrong with the flowers and my hair?" He nods. "Well, I had Tui find me a pounamu, you know, for some good juju. But..." I take a breath then slowly peel the dressing gown away from my neck. "I think I'm allergic to the leather it was on."

"Oh, baby." His eyes soften and he reaches a tentative hand out but pulls back before making contact. "That looks painful."

Tears well in my eyes, and I swipe them away. Apparently without my lucky knickers I've turned into a wuss too. "It stings like a bitch."

"We should get that looked at, so it doesn't get infected."

I hadn't even thought of that. It'll be just my luck to end up with oozy pus-filled welts on the biggest day of my life. I shake my head. "*We* aren't doing anything. *You* are going to play golf with Dylan and have a relaxing day."

"But—"

I touch a finger to his lips. "No buts. I've already messaged Marianne. Between her and Dallas we'll work something out." My phone pings beside me. "That'll be her now." I wave him off. "Go and get ready for your man-date."

"It's not a date."

"Potato, potahto." I grin up at him, trying to make it look like I'm not falling apart on the inside. "Go. I'll be fine."

"You sure?"

"Mmhmm. I'll see you tomorrow." I stand, careful not to jostle my gown against the welts and give him a kiss. "I'll be the one with the purple hair and a dying bunch of daisies." I snort out something like a half-cry, half-laugh. My bottom lip wobbles, and I suck it in so he doesn't see.

I have got to get a grip.

"I come bearing gifts!" Marianne sings out as she pushes her way through the door. "Dallas said this should clear it right up." She gasps when she finds me standing in the kitchen with my hair piled in a messy bun atop my head and an ice pack held to my neck. "Has it spread?"

I nod meekly, turning to her with red-rimmed eyes. "I'm a mess."

"Oh, honey." She drops her bag and the tube of cream and rushes to my side. "What can I do?"

"Find my damn knickers before I self-combust." I try to laugh but it comes out as a strangled cry. Marianne gapes, her mouth opening and closing like a goldfish.

She sniffs, then rolls up her sleeves. "Alright, I didn't want to have to do this, but it's time for some tough love." She places her hands on my upper arms—probably because the rash has spread across to my shoulders—and levels me with a stare. "You have got to snap out of this. The Susan I know wouldn't give two shits about a stupid pair of knickers, lucky or not. What's so damn special about this pair? Because for the length of time we've known each other, I've never once heard you talk about them. What's gotten into you? Is it nerves? You've changed your mind? What?"

I blink once, twice, then slump out of her grip and lean against the counter. "I know, okay? I know how stupid it sounds. But you *know* me, right? You know I never let any guy get under my skin until I met Gus. I was used to being the one in charge of my destiny, the one who made the rules and broke them when I wanted. I was used to not allowing… *feelings*—" I shudder, "—get in the way of having a romp in the sack. Until I met Gus."

"Right." She draws the word out. "I know all that, but what does that have to do with these knickers and the way you're letting them dictate your life right now? Because the Susan I know would never let a flimsy piece of material have so much power."

I huff out a sigh and drop the ice pack onto the bench. "You're going to think it's ridiculous."

"Um, you're talking to someone who frequently dresses like a clown and acts the fool in front of children. Believe me, I won't think it's ridiculous."

She's right. I know she is. I've seen her in that crazy get-up, and I watched her make a fool of herself to get Dallas back all those years ago, prancing around on his lawn. If anyone can understand this, it's Marianne.

"Okay, well, you see, I was wearing these knickers on the night I met Gus and took him home."

"Awww," she gushes, holding her hand to her chest, and I just about barf at how mushy this whole thing is. "Okay that's sweet."

"I was also wearing them on our second date. And when we got the message that you guys were adopting, I was wearing them too."

Her eyes well up, and I push on before the dam breaks.

"And when he proposed to me." I lift my hands and let them fall to my thighs. "So, you see? They've been there at all the important moments, and I'm scared that if I'm not wearing them, it won't happen."

Marianne takes my hands in hers. "You know what else was present at every one of those moments?" I stare blankly at her. "You."

I roll my eyes. "Well of course I was. I was the one wearing the knickers."

"So the knickers aren't the good luck, *you* are."

I huff out a laugh. "Yeah, cos I've been having great luck so far, haven't I?"

"It's all in your head. Stop thinking it's the knickers bringing you luck and start believing in yourself. Give me some of that *Susance* attitude." She snaps her fingers side-to-side. "You've totally got this!"

Chapter nine

I allowed myself to believe her when she said it was up to me. I even noticed an improvement in my rash when I woke this morning, which I took to be a good sign. However, that all went down the toilet when my makeup artist cancelled on me last minute because of some stupid bug she'd caught, so she was sending her apprentice.

I'm no snob. I'm as blue collar as they come, but when I open the door to see a woman who looks as if she stepped right out of the 80s on my doorstep, I don't know whether to laugh or cry.

"Hey." She waves and noisily pops the gum in her mouth. "Susan?"

I nod.

"I'm Barbie—" *of course you are* "—Kym's apprentice. I'm here to do your makeup." She waggles her eyebrows and jostles past me. "Where do you want me to set up?"

"Um, over there, I guess." I point her through to the kitchen where I see Marianne trying and failing to hide the *what the fuck* look she's sporting. I hear Tui chuckle in the other room, and the faintest "Get a perm," can be heard, followed by more laughter, and I can't help but join in. Barbie, if that's really her real name, has a perm that could rival Farrah Fawcet, enough blue eye shadow to sink a ship, and she's teetering on heels that look as though they'd snap if she turned too quickly.

Did I miss something? Are the 80s back in now? Is that why I've been seeing a ridiculous number of mullets walking around town? This is unacceptable. I thought I'd left that decade well behind. It was not a pretty time to be alive, and I don't know why anyone would want to relive it. So much spandex and fluorescent colour, and don't get me started on the high-waisted jeans.

"So what did you have in mind, doll? Something fun to go with that hair?" She plants her hand on her hip, tilting her head. "Love the colour, be-tee-dubs. Super-in right now."

"Uh, thanks, but I think I'll go with something a little more natural. You know, don't want to stand out too much." I widen my eyes and take the glass of wine Marianne is holding out to me with a grin.

Barbie snorts. "It's your big day, silly. You're meant to stand out. Trust me. I know exactly the right look for you."

Judging by her orange tan and sparkly false lashes, I highly doubt that.

"And what about you, ladies? What are you after?" She turns and points a long, pointed, ruby-red nail at Marianne and Tui. Their eyes widen, and they splutter. I grin as I take a hefty sip of my wine. That'll teach them to laugh at me. If I'm going to look like an 80s drag queen on my wedding day, they're going to join me.

"Oh that's okay, we can do our own, right, Tui?"

Tui waves a hand through the air. "Oh yeah, we're fine."

"Don't be silly, you two," I say in a sing-song voice. "That's what Barbie is here for. She's doing all three of us so we're matching." I look at them from behind Barbie's shoulder and mouth the words, "If I'm going down, so are you."

"Right." Barbie claps her hands. "Who's going first?"

###

"Maybe it'll look better once we're dressed," Marianne suggests as we stand in front of the bathroom mirror with another glass of wine. Our hair is beautifully twisted atop our heads, but everything farther south is not a pretty sight. Barbie did as she said she would. There's no way anyone could miss us with makeup this bold.

"I don't think there's anything, barring a paper bag, that will make this look any better." I take a sip of wine. "We look like we should be on stage singing *It's Raining Men.*"

"I don't know, girl, I kinda like it." Tui turns this way and that, swishing her robe about.

"Easy for you to say, you didn't get a foundation line across your neck." Marianne frowns, and I can't help but snigger. Granted, I look like a drag queen who's seen better days, but at least I'm not alone.

"It just needs blending. Here, let's have a look." Tui licks her finger and walks towards Marianne, who squeals and darts behind me.

"Don't you dare!"

"What's a little spit between friends?" I take a step to the side, leaving her exposed, and Tui lunges. Perhaps we need to ease up on the wines. At this rate, we won't make it in one piece.

"Alright, ladies." I hold my hands up, stepping between them. "As much as I want to see how this plays out, we don't have time." I swirl the dregs of wine in my glass and tip it back, placing the empty glass on the vanity. "We have an hour until the driver picks us up. Time to make me look as good as the Queen Bee herself."

Chapter ten

Fez, our limo driver, greets us with a jaunty step and a tip of his hat. He has me confirm the details and then ushers us into the back seats.

This thing is sleek and luxurious, and I feel like a movie star riding around town in it. It has soft leather seats and loads of leg room to spread out. There's a mini fridge filled with refreshments, and the windows are tinted black so no one can see in.

We do a quick circuit through town before making our way up to the Cashmere hills. We've been driving a mere fifteen minutes before Fez pulls to the side.

"I drop you here." He steps out of the car before I can say anything and opens our door, stepping back.

"Uh, no. This isn't the place."

"Yes. I drop you here," he says again, sniffing and looking at his watch.

"No, no. You take us to the venue. The Old Stone House in Cracroft." I point up the hill.

The driver clears his throat and shakes his head. "No, GPS says here is venue."

I climb over Marianne's lap to get out next to him. "Look around, Einstein. Does this look like a wedding venue to you?"

"Venue is here," he insists. "I drop you here."

"For shit's sake! Are you listening to me? This is not the venue!"

"I... uh..." He tugs at his collar, and a thin bead of sweat forms on his top lip. "GPS..."

I step into his personal space, peering up at him and poking a finger in his chest. "If you say this is the venue one more time..."

"Uh, Suz." Marianne grips my shoulders and pulls me away. "Stop scaring the guy." She pushes me back towards the car. "He clearly doesn't understand. I'll sort this."

I climb back into my seat and wait while she explains where we need to go. He keeps shaking his head, insisting we are in the right place. A quick glance at my phone shows we have a whole five minutes until we're meant to be there.

"Shit." I clamber back out again, motioning for Tui to follow suit. "Forget this. We don't have time. We'll walk."

Marianne stares at me. "In these heels?"

I gesture towards the retreating driver. "What choice do we have?" I bring up the map app on my phone and punch in the address. "Twenty minutes!" I look at my bridesmaids with a look of horror. "Gus is going to think I'm bailing on him."

"No, he won't. Just send him a message and let him know we ran into a snag and will be a bit late. He'll understand."

She's right, he will. He's that kind of guy. Me, on the other hand, I would be a basket case if the shoe was on the other foot. I need to try and invoke some of his calm temperament instead of my hot-headedness.

I flick a quick message to Gus, and Marianne lets Dallas know too, just in case. Then we pull our heels off, link arms, and trudge up the hill towards the venue.

Google Maps takes us on a tiki tour of the area, making us circle back on ourselves and, at one point, cross a small creek. My dress is a little worse for wear, droplets of mud clinging to the hem, and a grass stain up the back where I had a run-in with a dip in the ground on an embankment, but the end is in sight.

The Old Stone House looms closer, and tears well in my eyes as I realise I'm finally here. After the week from Hell, I finally made it to my wedding. I suck in large lungfuls of air, trying to calm my racing heart. It's actually going to—

"Suz? Is that you?" Gus's voice comes from the steps, and he runs towards us. "Thank God, I was starting to worry."

I quickly dart behind the girls, cowering. "No! Stop! You can't see me, it's bad luck."

His steps slow, and I peer through the gap between my friends. There he is, my husband to be, in his tailored tux, looking all kinds of sexy. It's enough to take my breath away, which it does. Everything I've been through this week has led me to this moment, and now that I'm here, I'm more than overwhelmed. I gasp, clutching a hand to my throat as I try to draw air in, but the harder I try, the harder it gets. Black spots dance in front of my eyes, and I feel myself falling to the ground in slow motion.

When I come to, I'm lying on my back with a swarm of faces in front of me. Dallas has his hand on my forehead, and both Marianne and Tui are standing behind him with worried expressions on their faces.

"Suz, baby, are you okay?" It's Gus, and he's holding my hand. I smile at him, until I realise where I am; on the ground behind The Old Stone House. My wedding venue. On my wedding day. With my fiancé looking down at me. The one person who shouldn't be seeing me yet.

"No! You shouldn't be here." I close my eyes, losing the fight with the tears in my eyes. "It's no use. I tried, Marianne. I tried to believe, but you're wrong. I'm the bringer of bad luck." I bring my hands up to swat at the tears streaming down my face. "He's seen me now. This is never going to work."

Gus glances up at Marianne, who nods, and everyone dissipates. It's just the two of us now. He helps me to sit, and we slump against one of the cars in the lot.

"You don't want to get married." It's more of a statement than a question.

"No." I shake my head. "I do. I want nothing more than to marry you, Gus, but I'm scared."

"Scared of what?"

"Scared that I'll screw it up. I've never done anything like this before, and I've never felt like this for anyone. I don't know how to do this without buggering it up."

He chuckles softly and takes my hand in his. "I don't know what I'm doing either. I just know that I want to be with you, and that I've never been more scared than I was just now when you had that panic attack."

I scoff. "That wasn't a panic attack."

"Yes, it was."

"No, it wasn't." I turn to look at him and see the concern on his face. "Okay, maybe I was a little bit panicked." I let my hand fall onto my lap. "I must look a right mess."

"You've never looked more beautiful to me."

I snort. "You've already got me, you don't need to keep trying."

"I'm not trying. I mean it." He brushes a wayward strand of hair from my face, and I raise a quizzical brow at him.

"I think you need your eyes tested. My dress is ruined, no thanks to that useless driver we had, my hair is all over the place, and it's frickin purple! And I look like I should be strutting about with Ru Paul." He chuckles. "Meanwhile, you're over here looking all dapper like you just stepped out of a GQ photoshoot. It's not fair."

He grabs the lapels of his jacket and puffs his chest out. "You like it, huh?"

"I love it."

"Enough to walk down the aisle with me?"

A fresh wave of tears fill my eyes. "Really? Even looking like this?" I gesture at my now tatty dress. "You'd still marry me?"

"Especially like this." He stands, then offers his hand. "What do you say? You wanna get married?"

"But... I don't understand. I'm not even wearing any knickers."

He clears his throat and gives a little chuckle. "Uh, I'm not sure what that has to do with getting married, but I'm definitely going to be thinking about it for the rest of the evening." He looks down at me with a hint of playfulness, pulling me in to plant a kiss on my lips. And it's then it hits me. It wasn't the knickers that were lucky, it was *him*. Gus was my lucky star all along, and lucky me, I get to marry him.

"So? How about it?" He tilts his head towards the guests milling about, trying not to look as though they're watching the hot mess that is me.

Lady Luck

I smooth my hands down the front of his chest. "It would be a shame to let that suit go to waste."

"So that's a yes then?"

I nod, linking my arm through his. "It's a yes. Let's get hitched!"

Chapter eleven

The opening notes of *Crazy in Love* blare through the speakers, and Marianne, clutching Toby's hand, struts her way down the aisle. A few beats later, Tui follows suit, joining them up the front with Gus, who stands with his hands folded in front of him, and the biggest grin on his face.

I suck in a deep breath, then hold my bouquet up high while I wiggle my hips and sashay my way down the petal-strewn walkway. Our guests clap in time to the beat, but it's all background noise to me. I can't take my eyes off the man I'm about to marry. He steps towards me, his arms held out, and I slide my way into his embrace.

"You look beautiful." He winks, taking my hands in his and leading me to where the celebrant is waiting.

She smiles warmly, then clears her throat and addresses the congregation. "We are gathered here today, to celebrate the joining of two souls. Susan Marie Phillips and Angus Dean Callaghan.

"Your wedding is a public proclamation of your love and commitment made here in front of your family and friends. But more than that, it is a promise to each other. A promise that will be the foundation of your life together.

"Marriage gives a permanence and structure to a couple's love. It's a way to tell one another that no matter how much you snore or how much you dance around like Beyoncé, you're in this together."

She pauses while the congregation chuckles, then motions for Marianne to step forward. I turn to face her as she unfolds a piece of paper.

"I felt this was a fitting poem for these two. Love you guys." She makes an *ahem* noise in the back of her throat.

"I take you as my husband,
For all the world to see.
I'll cherish you forever,
If you'll only cherish me.
I'll be your one and only,
Till death unto us part.
You'll never be without me,
For it's you who holds my heart.
I take you as my husband,
To be the one I call,
Who fixes all the things,
And lifts me when I fall.
I'll try to cook you dinner,
And you can buy the wine,
And if you're feeling lucky,
I'll show you a good time.
Yes, I take you as my husband,

I'll put a ring on you,
There's nothing more to say except,
I do, I do, I do!"

She folds the paper and tucks it under the strap of her dress before stepping back beside Tui. Her hand lands on the top of Toby's head, giving his hair a gentle ruffle.

The celebrant nods. "Thank you, Marianne." She turns back to the front. "And now Susan and Gus will read their own vows." She tips her head towards me. "Susan."

I inhale sharply through my nose then huff it out, giving my head a shake. "Okay, here goes."

Gus chuckles, giving my hands a squeeze of encouragement.

"Gus, I promise to love and cherish you always, and I'll obey maybe fifty percent of the time."

There's a smatter of laughter in the pews, and Gus has a goofy grin on his face.

"I promise to let you hold the remote, as long as I can choose the movie. I promise to pretend to listen to you talk about sports or beer or whatever builders talk about and nod as if I'm paying attention.

"For real though, Gus, you are my one and only. The yin to my yan. The Yoda to my Luke." I grimace, whispering, "Did I get that one right?"

He laughs and nods. "Yes, you got that right."

"You are the one I want to fall asleep with at night and wake up to in the morning. You are my lucky star, and I love you with all my heart."

"Aww." Marianne's voice chimes from behind me, followed by a loud nose blow into a tissue. I turn to her with a raised brow, and she holds her hand up. "Sorry. As you were."

"Gus?" the celebrant prompts.

"Right. Hard to follow up on that one, but I'll give it a nudge.

"Suz, from the moment I laid eyes on you, I knew you were it for me. It took you a little longer to figure that out, and a lot of persistence from me, but we got there in the end.

"I promise to love and cherish you always, knickers or no knickers."

An unladylike snort bursts from me as I laugh, and Tui cackles beside Marianne.

"I promise to never watch the next episode without you, or at least to pretend I didn't when we watch it together. I promise to always let you choose the music in the car, even if I have to listen to Beyoncé for six hours straight."

"Now that's love," someone shouts from down the back.

"It sure is, brother," Gus replies. "Suz, you are my world. I can't imagine spending my life without you by my side. I love you, baby."

I sniff and wipe a finger under my eye before the thick mascara can careen down my face and make me look even worse for wear.

"Susan, do you take this man to be your lawfully wedded husband, to have and to hold, in sickness and in health, in sorrow and in joy, from this day forward, as long as you both shall live?"

"Hell yes, I do!"

"And you, Gus, do you take this woman to be your lawfully wedded wife, to have and to hold, in sickness and in health, in sorrow and in joy, from this day forward, as long as you both shall live?"

"I absolutely do."

"And now the rings." The celebrant beckons Toby to the front, and after a little nudge from Marianne, he obliges. He stands between us, holding the white cushion up with a grin. I wink, and he grins wider.

"Gus, I give you this ring as a symbol of my love, with the pledge to love you today, tomorrow, always and forever." I slide the ring onto his finger, then he takes the next ring from the cushion.

"Susan, I give you this ring as a symbol of my love, with the pledge to love you today, tomorrow, always and forever." My heart thunders in my chest as he places the ring on my finger, and I stare at the sparkling diamond twinkling in the sunlight.

This is it. We actually did it.

We made it.

Lady Luck

I'm Mrs. Susan Callaghan!

The celebrant closes her book and clasps her hands in front of her. "Before these witnesses, you have pledged to be joined in marriage. You have sealed that pledge with these rings. And now, by the authority vested in me, I now pronounce you husband and wife. You may kiss the bride."

There's a woop and a cheer from our families and friends as Gus steps forward, wraps his arms around me, and lowers me into a dip, pressing his lips to mine.

Chapter twelve

Marianne stands, clinking her glass. "I'd like to make a toast to the bride and groom." She raises her glass. "Suz has been a permanent fixture in my life for more years than I can count. She's always had my back, and she's certainly kept things interesting. If it wasn't for her antics, Dallas and I would never have met—"

I snort, interrupting her. "I want the record to show I had *nothing* to do with *that* particular meeting." I waggle my brows, lifting my glass to my lips.

Marianne's face turns a brilliant shade of red and she clears her throat. "Okay, we wouldn't have *reconnected* then without the meddling of Suz." She pretends to glare at me, but the curve to her lips gives her away. "And I'll forever be grateful to her for that." She smiles down at Dallas, and he takes her hand, bringing it to his lips. "I wasn't sure I'd see the day when Suz would finally walk down the aisle and join us in wedded bliss, but here we are. I knew as soon as she mentioned him, that Gus was a gamechanger." She turns to him with a grin. "You've got your hands full with this one, but I'm sure you know that already." She chuckles as he nods his head. "Gus, you balance out her craziness and clearly have the patience of a saint." Laughter floats around the room. "Honestly though, I am honoured to share this day with you two. Without Suz in my life, it would've been a dull existence, and I know she's found her match in you." She glances around the room. "To the bride and groom!"

"To the bride and groom!" everyone repeats, tipping their glasses back.

Gus pushes his seat back and stands. "Thank you, Marianne." He tips his glass in her direction. "And might I say, you ladies look," he clears his throat, "delightful today."

Tui snorts, and Marianne rolls her eyes.

"Susan might've needed a little time to come to terms with the fact we were meant to be, but I knew from the moment I saw her. She was the loudest one in the room, both in sound and personality, and I knew she was the one for me."

"I can't say I blame you. I'm quite the catch," I add with a smirk.

He chuckles. "You certainly are. That's why I had to put a ring on it." He winks, and I can't help but laugh. This man gets me better than anyone. "Suz, you are *irreplaceable*, and you've got me so *crazy in love* with you. I can't wait to spend the rest of our lives hearing you *say my name* with yours." There's a mix of groans and laughter across the room, and a few puzzled expressions, but all I can do is grin up at him. "Love you, babe." He raises his glass. "To *Susancé*, my queen."

"*Susancé*!" Glasses clink together, and everyone starts chatting amongst themselves.

I wrap my arm around Gus and lean my head on his shoulder. "Have I told you how much I love you?"

"Not nearly enough times today," he jokes, planting a kiss atop my head. "And the feeling is mutual, which is a good thing considering we just got hitched. Otherwise, this is one hell of an expensive party."

I slap his chest playfully. "Worth every penny."

There's a glint in his eye, and he pulls his lips in tight before saying, "Sure, until all those *bills, bills, bills* start rolling in."

"How many more of these do you have tucked up your sleeve?" I ask with a grin. "Did you Google every single song she's ever done?"

"I'm nothing if not thorough. Attention to detail is part of the job as a builder, you know."

"I'm sure it is. And I bet all your builder pals will be thoroughly impressed with your Beyoncé knowledge." I accept another glass from a passing waiter and lift it to my lips.

"You joke, but they wanted to do a flashmob dance thing." He shakes his head. "I love you, but that's going a bit far."

Just then the first beats of *Love on Top* blast through the speakers, and two of his friends leap to their feet, clicking their fingers in time.

My mouth drops open. "Whaaaat?" I giggle, covering my mouth as more stand and make their way to the centre of the room. "You didn't…"

Gus throws his napkin down on the table, jumping up and wiggling his hips as he points at me, singing, "Baby it's you!" He spins and shimmies his way to the group of men who are now doing the old backing-singer-step-together dance, complete with finger clicks and synchronised turns. Gus sways in the middle, mouthing all the words into a microphone that Dallas hands him before joining in with the others. Even Tony is in on it.

I look to the girls. "You knew about this?"

They both shake their heads, staring in amazement at their husbands gyrating before them.

"I've never seen Dallas pull out moves like that!" Marianne hoots, getting to her feet and clapping.

Tui whistles loudly. "Yeah! Shake it, baby!"

The music changes to something a bit slower, and Ed Sheeran's voice begins singing *Perfect*. Gus crooks his finger at me, and I make my way over to him. My nose tingles, and a tear forms in my eye as he wraps his arms around me, and we sway to the music right as Beyoncé begins her part.

I rest my head against his chest, letting him lead me around the room. The perfect guy, with the perfect song, and the perfect day. I'd had my doubts when it was one disaster after another, but Gus, and all our friends, have made this so much more than I could've imagined.

Lady Luck

Chapter thirteen

Just before midnight, Marianne taps me on the shoulder and suggests we make a move so she and Tui can start the clean-up as per the room hire agreement. If I'm honest, it's been an exhausting day, and I'm about ready to pack it in anyway, so I find Gus and we say our goodbyes.

The cab ride to our hotel is quiet. His mother put us up in a swanky hotel at the top of the hill, and I'm excited to see what it looks like. We pull up outside A View from the Top and the front door opens, a woman rushing up to greet us.

"Hi, you two lovebirds," she gushes. "I'm Sierra, the owner of this establishment. Come, come. Your bags are already in your room." She ushers us towards the door and into a brightly lit hall. "You've got the place to yourselves this evening. My husband and I stay on the lower floor, but you won't hear a peep from us." She grins back at us as she marches up the stairs and to the end of another hall, where she unlocks a door. Swinging it open, she waves her hand like a gameshow hostess.

I follow Gus, my eyes drinking in the elaborately decorated room, complete with a large king size bed in the centre of the room, a plush rug at the foot of the bed, and an already glowing fireplace. Flowing curtains billow in the cool night air coming from the wall-sized window overlooking the twinkling lights of the city below.

"The bathroom is through that door, and if you'll follow me…" She hurries to the window, revealing a large ranch slider. Sweeping the curtains back, she steps out onto the patio. "I took the liberty of heating the spa for you, and if you're so inclined, you can switch off the lighting to get a clearer view over the city." She hands a remote to Gus. "When you're ready in the morning, come on down to the kitchen and I'll prepare your breakfast. Your mother booked eggs benedict with bacon. I hope that's okay."

My stomach growls at the mention of food, and Sierra lets out a light laugh. "You two make yourselves at home, and I'll rustle up a platter of snacks for you." She turns on her heels and marches back out, pulling the door closed behind her.

"I have to say, your mother has outdone herself," I say, staring wide-eyed at the city I've lived in my whole life. "It's beautiful up here."

"It sure is." Gus tucks a strand of hair behind my ear and nestles his head in the crook of my shoulder. "Shall we try out the spa?"

His lips tickle against my neck, and I shrug my shoulders upwards as goosebumps cover my skin. It drives me crazy when he does that, and he knows it. "You'll have to help me out of this dress first." I take a step back, turning away from him. Tugging the pins from my hair, I let it fall loose around my shoulders as I glance back at him. "Unhook me?"

His eyes seem to devour me as he swallows. His fingers brush lightly against the bare skin of my back as he gently moves to unfasten each separate hook. It's devastatingly slow and sensual, and my body shivers beneath his touch.

As he reaches the last hook, I shimmy my hips, letting the dress fall to the floor. Gus circles his hands around my waist, and I lean back into him. There's something so erotic about standing on top of the world, naked, with my husband's hands on me.

I can't help but smile. *My husband.*

That's going to take some getting used to.

"You seem to be over dressed, *husband,*" I say as I slip from his grasp and saunter towards the spa. Kicking my heels to the side, I climb the step and sink into the deliciously warm water, settling myself against the far side. From here I can see the whole city, and it's magical.

Gus makes quick work of removing his tux, folding it haphazardly and dumping it on a nearby seat. As he steps into the water, a low moan falls from his lips. "This is incredible."

I eye him with a hunger that hasn't diminished in all our years together. Curling my finger, I beckon him closer. My arms wrap around his neck as he lifts me to straddle his lap. His lips are soft and sensuous as he plants light kisses over mine. I wrap my arms tighter, pulling him into me. My hips rock against his, a gentle rhythm that matches the play of his tongue duelling with mine.

He hisses out a sharp breath as I raise my hips and position myself over him. Slowly lowering myself, I savour the feel of his warmth throbbing inside me.

Our kisses become fervent, our hands exploring each other's bodies until we reach a fever pitch. Tossing my head backwards, I buck my hips faster, clutching at his shoulders, needing everything he has to give me. His lips find purchase on my nipple, and as his teeth softly bite down, my release explodes around him. I cry out in ecstasy, my body no longer able to move of its own accord. Gus clamps his hands down on my hips, taking over. My fingers twine in his hair, my lips crushing to his as I ride it out. Already I can feel it building to another crescendo, and I will myself to hold on a little longer.

"Oh fuck," Gus hisses as his hips begin lifting feverishly.

I squeeze my forearms around his neck, holding myself in place so I can once again take control. My hips slide over his, hitting that spot just right.

"Oh baby." Gus presses his forehead to mine, our breaths mingling.

"I'm... almost..." I pant, closing my eyes as I feel it rising inside. "So... close..." Our bodies collide with a need so strong, so desperate, and then... sweet release.

"Fuck!" I cry out, clamping my thighs around his waist. "Holy shit." My head falls to his shoulder, my heart thudding in my chest.

Gus wraps his arms around my waist, his lips kissing slowly up the side of my neck. "If I'd known married sex was going to be this great, I would've asked you a lot sooner."

Chapter fourteen

The next morning, I wake with the ache of a night well spent. After our little spa rendezvous, we returned to the bedroom for another round, followed by a nibble on the platter Sierra had left on the table for us. I'm not sure when she'd left it there, but I'm sure she would have had a pretty good show when she did.

Rolling to my side, I take in Gus's sleeping features. The light dusting of stubble on his chin, the way wisps of his hair fall softly over his ear, and the smirk slowly appearing the longer I stare. "Having a good look, wifey?" He opens one eye, and his lips pull into a full-blown smile.

I trail my finger along his jawline, listening to the sound my nail makes on his stubble. "Mmhmm."

He rolls to face me, draping his arm across my waist. "Are you ready for our next adventure?"

"If by next adventure you mean morning marital sex, then yes. Yes I am." I run my tongue along my top teeth with a frown. "Hold that thought. Let me go brush my teeth real quick."

He chuckles, tugging me against him as he buries his face in the crook of my neck. "I'm not saying no, but that wasn't what I was meaning."

"It wasn't?" I don't even try to hide the disappointment in my voice.

He pulls back, tucking two fingers beneath my chin and tilting my face to meet his. He presses his lips to mine once, twice, then three times. "I was meaning our honeymoon. But I'm all for morning marital sex too." He runs his hands over my curves. "Is that something I can expect every day?"

"If you play your cards right."

"I knew I was going to enjoy being married to you." He grins, planting a kiss to my forehead.

I snort. "It's not really all that different from before. We still had a lot of sex."

"But not morning sex. That's the best time for it." He thrusts his hips against mine, showing me exactly what he's meaning.

"Well, it would be a shame to waste it." I reach down to grip him in my hand, the silky soft skin hot to the touch. He lets out a throaty growl, and his eyes flutter closed.

I shuffle in closer, nudging him onto his back. Kicking the sheets off, I kneel beside him, one brow arched in question.

"Oh, please, baby," he urges, his hips lifting to meet each stroke. I lower my head until my lips hover over him, my breath teasing the sensitive skin around his tip. He bucks against my lips as I press soft kisses along his length before dragging my tongue from tip to base. He hisses out a breath, cursing softly.

Licking my lips, I take hold of the base, slowly stroking up and down as I lower my lips around him. He lets out a low moan, his hands twisting through my hair. I swirl my tongue over the ridges, and his hand forms a fist in my hair, pulling it taught.

With my hand still pumping, I take him to the back of my throat before slowly pulling back. Moving quickly, I straddle his hips, lining him up and sinking down. We both let out a groan of pleasure as he slides in to the hilt. With my hands braced on his chest, and his hands firmly grasping my hips, I start to move; rocking slowly at first. His fingers dig into my flesh, but it only spurs me on, my hips grinding, chasing that high I know is not far away.

I claw at his chest, my breath coming in short pants as I speed up. His hands find their way to my breasts, and he lifts his head to meet them. With one hand massaging, his mouth latches on to the other, flicking, teasing.

Cupping my hands to his jaw, I drag his lips to mine to swallow the moan forming as I begin to peak. His hands slide back to my hips, guiding me in a frenzied pace until I'm barely breathing anymore. With one final thrust, he grips my hips, and I fall to pieces, crying out his name.

I wrap my legs around his waist, cradling his head against my chest as a grin starts to form. "Do you think they heard us?"

"You, you mean? Do I think they heard you?" He turns his amused gaze to mine. "I think the whole neighbourhood did." He waggles his brows, cocking his head to the side. "From what I'm told, it's not the first time either. And at least this time you had company." His shoulders shake as he laughs.

If it wasn't so adorable seeing him amused at my past indiscretions, I'd kill Marianne for spilling my secrets. What a girl does in the privacy of her best friend's spare bedroom is sacred. So what if it could be heard down the street?

Once we're showered and dressed, we head down to the kitchen where Sierra is already bustling about. "Morning, lovebirds," she sings. "There's coffee on the counter, and I'm just about to start on the bacon. Any other requests?"

I take a seat at the breakfast bar and pour two mugs of coffee, adding extra sugar to mine.

"This is lovely, Sierra, thank you." Gus takes the proffered mug and moves to stand by the window, checking out the view in daylight. "It's a beautiful place you have here."

"Oh thank you." She smiles, turning her back to the stove. "My husband and I used to run a bed and breakfast many years ago, but we decided to try something different, a little more upmarket." She gestures to the opulent living quarters. "And as soon as we saw this place, we fell in love." She turns back to the sizzling pan, flipping the bacon over. "We like to offer a taste of luxury, and we tend to get a lot of honeymooners, or anniversary dates here."

"I can see why. The views are spectacular, and that spa…" Gus sighs, rocking back on his heels. "That was something else."

"Oh, I know." She winks, giving me a knowing smile. "It's one of our most popular features."

I snort, nearly spilling my coffee. So she had received an unsolicited peep show last night then. If the tables were turned, I don't think I could behave quite so diplomatically. In fact, I know I couldn't. It's not in me to ignore a chance to give a good ribbing. Even if I don't know the person from a bar of soap.

I catch Gus's eye with a quirk of my brow, and his cheeks redden. He's used to my antics, but this is the first time he's been part of my indiscretions.

To her credit, Sierra notices his discomfort and switches back to chef mode, hiding the smirk on her lips as she ducks down, pulling another pan from the cupboard. She places it on the stovetop then turns to us, brushing her hands down her front.

"Now, how do you like your eggs?"

Chapter Fifteen

Bags loaded into the car, we set off on our road trip to Hanmer Springs for the next five days. The days leading up to our wedding was so stressful, I can't wait to visit the thermal pools and really relax. I've booked us a couple's pamper package that includes a one-hour massage each, a soak in the private pools, and a facial treatment for me while he hits the sauna. It's going to be bliss.

"How're we going for time? I booked us in for three o'clock, and I don't want to be a hot, sweaty mess when we arrive." I bite the end off a strap of liquorice before offering it to him.

"Not too much farther. We're nearly at Frog Rock." He nods his head towards a collection of limestone rocks balanced on the side of a small rise.

I squint my eyes, tilting my head. "I don't see it."

He points. "See that bit? That's the head. It looks better from the other side."

There's a small building beneath it with the words 'Frog Rock' painted in bold. I can't imagine it being so popular it needs that kind of an announcement. It *is* just a bunch of rocks.

I continue staring at it as it looms closer, still not seeing the resemblance, but as we pass, I swivel in my seat, and there it is. A ginormous frog-shaped rock.

"That's actually pretty neat." I turn back to the front. "Who'd have thought?"

Gus chuckles. "You'd be surprised how many people stop to take pictures. It's quite the tourist spot." He glances out the corner of his eye at me. "I can't believe you've never been out here before."

I shrug, folding my hands in my lap. "I'm a city girl through and through. What would I want to see a bunch of rocks for?"

"You never just went for a drive for the hell of it in your younger days?"

It's my time to side-eye him. "*Younger* days? *I am still in my prime*, thank you very much."

His palm settles on my thigh, giving it a squeeze. "Of course you are."

We make our way through winding roads, up and down the valleys, and over a rickety bridge used for bungy jumping. It barely seems safe enough for just our car to drive over, there's no way you'd catch me diving headfirst off the side of it. I like a challenge and a bit of adventure as much as the next girl, but that is where I draw the line. The view alone is dizzying.

Before long, we round the bend to see the sign welcoming us to Hanmer Springs. Gus slows the car as we coast down the tree-lined main road of the quaint village. It's a popular tourist destination, and there are plenty of cars around to prove it.

He pulls up outside the Rental Homes reception, collects our key, and then we make our way partially up Conical Hill to our street. Number 27 is a petite bungalow with a small wooden verandah and a turret off the front room.

Inside is cosy. It's an open plan living/kitchen area with a bay window overlooking the driveway. Two plush chairs with matching two-seater couch line the walls, and a log fire stands in the corner.

Bedrooms on either side of the narrow hall each hold a queen bed with fluffy pillows and a lovely mink blanket folded at the end. I enter the first one, flopping down on the bed to check how it moves beneath me; does it have suitable *bounce*?

Gus walks in with a grin. "I know what you're thinking, but we don't have time if you want to make our reservation."

I scrunch my nose, but he's right. I don't want to miss it. "Just give me a minute to grab what I need." Unzipping my bag, I rummage through my clothes in search of my brand-new bikini bought especially for this trip. As soon as my eyes landed on the yellow polka dot bikini in the store, I knew I had to have it. And, as luck would have it, it goes nicely with my purple hair too.

I toss them into a smaller bag, along with my purse, phone, and a towel. A quick glance out the window tells me we might be in for some dicey weather later, so I grab my hoodie, just to be safe. As I refold it to fit inside my bag, I notice something bulging from inside the sleeve. I give it a squeeze. It feels like a balled-up sock. Unfolding the top, I shove my arm into the sleeve and pull out a scrunched-up ball of red fabric. My heart pitter patters, and I let out a squeal. "Oh my god, I found them!" I turn to Gus, rushing to untangle the lump in my hand. "My lucky knickers! They were here all along!" I thrust my hand up in the air, waving the unfurled knickers with glee. The unbridled excitement at having found them is ridiculous I know, especially after realising I had my very own good luck charm in Gus, but part of me still believes in the bloody things. "I must've been wearing them the day we went out to visit the venue and confirm; the day we went for a walk around Hagley Park and I got covered in pollen. I haven't worn this hoodie since then." I crush the silly things to my chest in a loving embrace. "I can't believe I forgot about that."

"And I can't believe you're tearing up over a pair of knickers." Gus chuckles, taking me in his arms.

I swipe a finger beneath my eye. "It's a momentous occasion. I thought I'd lost them forever."

"Well, unless those lucky knickers are going to keep you warm on the walk back after, I suggest you put them aside, and we can celebrate later." He plucks them from my hand and tosses them on the bed. "We have a date with a massage table."

###

After a wonderful afternoon of pampering, we head for a retro burger joint we'd seen on our walk into town. It looks like it belongs in the Buddy Holly era, with red vinyl booths, black and white tiled floors, and a jukebox playing songs from the 50s.

We each order a hamburger with cheesy fries and a shake. Settling into one of the booths, we go over our plan for the coming days.

"I've heard the walk up Conical Hill is quite nice." Gus says as he tugs a fry loose from the melted cheese.

I give him a sceptical look. "Have you forgotten who you married?"

Chuckling, Gus draws my attention to the hill we're sitting at the base of. "It's not that high. It won't even take us an hour to reach the top." He reaches over, palming my arm and jostling me. "Live a little."

"I've lived plenty, and trekking up a muddy hill is not my idea of fun." I pause, tearing my burger in half. "I mean, do these nails look like they belong on a hike?" I wiggle my sauce-covered fingers in his direction, and he grabs my hand, his lips forming a seal around the tips of my fingers. I lose all train of thought as his swirling tongue conjures up images of what I'd like to do to him later. "But I suppose, for you, I could give it a go," I mumble, fighting the urge to go all Meg Ryan in *When Harry met Sally.*

Gus pulls my fingers from between his lips with a pop and a grin before tucking back into the fries. His eyes latch onto something behind me, and they light up. "What about one of those?" He points, and I turn to see a man and woman sitting in the front of what looks to be a pedal drawn carriage. Their two children sit in the back seat, happily watching the world go by as their parents pump their legs in tandem to keep the thing moving. "It'd be a good way to see the area."

I scrunch my nose. "Looks like hard work. Can't we just lazily stroll around the streets by day and have kinky sex by night?"

His eyes smoulder as they turn to me. "I like the sound of that too." Dusting his hands on a napkin, he glances at his watch. "Oh, look at the time." He feigns a yawn then darts out of the booth and over to the counter.

"You really don't know me at all, do you?" I eye the uneaten food, then raise a brow at him.

"Can we get this to go please?" he asks the girl behind the counter, and she ducks down to retrieve a sheet of cardboard that she deftly folds into a takeaway box.

"Here you go." She smiles, handing it over. Gus pays the bill then hurriedly packs our food away.

"We're going to need this for sustenance later," he growls as he takes my hand and leads me back to our bungalow.

Chapter sixteen

The next morning I unhook my freshly washed lucky knickers from the hanging clothes rack, ready to put them to use. If I'm going to climb this blasted hill, I'm going to need all the luck I can get. Me and Mother Nature don't always see eye to eye, and it can get a little hairy sometimes. We came to an understanding many years ago, that I wouldn't attempt the outdoorsy lifestyle, and she would, in turn, leave me be.

The things we do for love though, right?

I pull on the only pair of pants I deem appropriate for such an endeavour; jeggings. And the ensemble is completed with a singlet, my hoodie, and my hair pulled back with a band. I didn't think to bring any kind of sports shoe with me, so I have to settle for my pink velveteen street shoes tied up with ribbons.

Gus raises a brow when he sees what I'm wearing, but he regards his life too highly to make a comment. "Ready to go then?" he asks instead.

"I think so. Will we need to take food with us?"

Chuckling, Gus guides me with a hand to the small of my back. "You know, most people would ask if we need to take water on a hike, not food."

I roll my eyes. "I think we both know I'm not like most people." I stop at the door. "So it's a no on the food then?"

"It's a no on the food."

"Okay," I draw the word out. "I hope you're right, because you know I get hangry."

"Believe me, I know," he says with a pained expression on his face. One that is met with a friendly backhand to the arm.

We head down the road and turn the corner to begin our trek. We've only been a few steps and already I can feel my chest tightening and my breaths are coming out in sharp pants.

"I thought you said this was going to be easy?" I brace my hands on my thighs as I suck in a breath.

"It will be. We just have to get up this part first."

He marches on, his long legs taking strides I can't compete with. We come to a dirt staircase, and I breathe a sigh of relief. This I can handle.

Once we reach the top, the trees form a canopy above us, and the path becomes wider and levelled out.

"See?" Gus takes my hand. "It's not so bad, right?"

If I'm honest, it's not. It's surprisingly pleasant walking hand-in-hand along the leaf-strewn pathway that winds slowly up the hill. At each bend there is a seat to rest, and some overlook the village and the surrounding area.

We make it to the top in far less time than I imagined it would take, and I've barely broken a sweat. My feet, however, are screaming at me. Street shoes are not made for all this up and down, rough walking business.

Despite my aching feet, I circle the viewing platform, taking in the sights. Behind us is another, higher hill lush with trees, and below is a patchwork of colour. It's quite beautiful.

Gus wraps his arms around me, resting his chin on my shoulder. "What do you think?"

"Okay, fine. It was actually kinda fun," I admit with a hint of sarcasm in my tone. I can't let him off too easily or he'll expect more of this from me, and I don't think my feet could take it.

"You ready to head back down?"

I nod. "Sure." I walk across the wooden structure leading to the platform and down over a cluster of rocks to the beginning of the path. A small wooden sign catches my eye, and I clamber across to read it. "Hey." I turn to Gus. "There's another path down. Shall we try it?"

His enthusiasm for my suggestion proves how much he's wanting me to enjoy this outdoorsy crap, but really, I'm just hoping for a quicker way home so I can get these shoes off.

The track is a little steeper than I expected, and there's little to no tread on my shoes, so I find myself almost skating down sections of the hill. Gus, to his credit, does his best to steady me, but I land on my butt multiple times.

We come to a point in the path where it seems to abruptly stop. There's a formation of rocks to one side, a steep embankment to the other, and thick trees in front of us.

Swivelling around, I look behind us. "Did we take a wrong turn somewhere?"

"I don't think so." Gus scratches his head. "Maybe we're meant to go down there." He points at the abrupt decline, and I gape at him.

"You've got to be shitting me. Did you see how many times I fell up there?" I shake my head, folding my arms across my chest. "Nuh-uh. I'm not doing it." My stomach grumbles loudly, reminding me I haven't eaten since we left, and that felt like hours ago.

"Unless you want to turn back the way we came, I don't think we have any other option, babe." Gus places his hand on my arm in what he thinks is a calming way, but all it does is fuel my hanger.

"Great. Just great." I throw my arms in the air, shaking him off. "We're lost. Out in the wilderness, and no one knows where we are." My voice cracks, and I swipe angrily at the tears that like to show their face when I'm beyond hungry. I knew I should've brought a snack with me.

"Babe," Gus says gently, taking me in his arms. "Everything will be fine. We can't have strayed too far. It's not like it's a mountain range."

His attempts are doing nothing to soothe me. My stomach is practically eating itself, my heels have blisters, my arse feels bruised from all the falls, and now, if I want to get out of this place alive, I've got to go bush? And not even in the good way.

Pulling from his embrace, I wipe the sleeve of my hoodie across my face before shaking my arms out. "Fine," I growl. "I'll do it, but then no more of this walking bullshit, okay?"

His lips quirk up in the corners, but he quickly pulls them into a straight line as he nods his agreement.

I grasp hold of a spindly tree trunk and take a cautious step down the slope. Twisting my body to the side, I edge down on an angle to give myself a better grip.

So far so good.

I make it down to the first flat and scan the area. There's another winding path leading back to where we came from, and a narrow one leading farther down. I take that one.

We walk for another half hour before finally breaking through to daylight. I breathe a sigh of relief at being out of the shadows, but a quick look around reveals we're not out of the woods yet.

Lush green grass surrounds us, fluffy white balls of fuzz graze in groups, and in the distance, a house. "Are we in someone's paddock?"

Chapter seventeen

The simple answer is yes. Yes, we are in a paddock. A paddock belonging to a disgruntled farmer—if you can call one lone paddock a farm that is—and his flock of sheep. I hear him before I see him, but it doesn't take a rocket scientist to realise he doesn't appreciate us traipsing across his land.

Gus grasps my hand. "Come on," he hisses as he nigh on drags me towards the road in the distance.

I'm dodging 'parcels' left, right, and bloody centre as I try to keep up with his long stride, and by the time we reach the road, I'm on the verge of collapse.

My lungs are crying out for air, that I suck in like it's going out of fashion, my thighs are burning from all the running and dodging, and my stomach chooses now to remind me it's fast running out of fuel.

Looking left to right, I can't get my bearings. "Where do we go from here?" I whine, wanting nothing more than to curl up in a ball and not move a muscle for the rest of the day. Unless that muscle is my jaw and I'm chewing on something tasty.

Gus rakes his hand across his forehead, his nose scrunched up as he turns both ways. "I think it's this way," he says with very little conviction, but at this point, I don't even care.

We trudge along the road, our feet barely lifting off the ground with each step. After ten minutes of walking, the houses begin to look familiar. By some miracle, we managed to get lost and still wind up on our street. And when I see the turret of our bungalow, I almost burst into tears. I could kiss the ground I'm so happy.

My stomach kicks up the growling, sensing food is imminent, and this time I'm the one encouraging Gus to move faster.

He unlocks the door, and we practically fall through, both making a beeline for the kitchen. Gus grabs a water bottle from the fridge and guzzles it down, while I head straight for the pantry, ripping open a pack of chips and shoving a handful into my mouth.

My shoulders loosen and I tip my head back, delighting in the pure pleasure of feeding my face.

"Well that was an adventure, wasn't it?" Gus says with enthusiasm and not a hint of sarcasm.

"That's one word for it I suppose," I mumble, taking my chips to the couch and flopping down. I can think of several other words I'd use instead of adventure. Disaster, debacle, fiasco, epic fail, to name a few.

Without bending down, I manage to flick both shoes across the floor and wriggle my toes, letting out a pained sigh.

"Sore feet?" Gus asks. You can't get anything past him.

"Mmm." With all the strength I can muster, I bring my legs up to lay along the couch, resting the packet of chips on my thighs.

Lifting my feet, Gus slides onto the couch beside me, placing my ankles on his lap. His fingers deftly press into the soles of my feet, working out the aches. I throw my head back in wanton abandonment, a moan slipping from my lips.

"God that feels good."

"I bet I can make the rest of you feel good too." He grins mischievously, and I stare at him with narrowed eyes.

"Alright, who are you and what have you done with my gentleman husband?" I hold up my hand, palm out. "Not that I'm complaining." In all honesty, I kind of like this newfound playfulness of his. It's downright sexy.

His lips quirk up to one side as he tilts his head. "What do you mean?"

"Oh nothing, just—" I gesture towards him, "—you're not normally so… forward. And, like I said, I'm not complaining. In fact—" I drag my feet from his lap and curl my body into his, "—I find it very sexy."

The mischievous glint is back in his eye. "Oh you do, do you?" He clears his throat. "Maybe you should show me just *how* sexy you find it."

"I think I can handle that," I purr, stroking a finger up and down his chest. With my lip pulled between my teeth, I deftly lift his top up and over his head, tossing it on the floor. Leaning down, I lap at his nipple as my fingers find the waistband of his pants.

His moan is guttural, primal, and it urges me on. My lips trail kisses down his chest and abdomen as I slide my body down to the floor, removing his pants and boxers as I go. His cock springs out to greet me, and I plant a kiss on the tip before standing to disrobe. In time to the beat in my head, I sway my hips as I discard my hoodie and slowly pull my top over my head. I turn my back to him, glancing over my shoulder as I shimmy my jeggings down my legs, keeping my knees locked in place to give him a good view.

"Now I see why you call them lucky," he murmurs as his hands cup my behind still wrapped in the lucky knickers. His breath is hot against my back, his lips brushing feather-light kisses across my skin.

I step out of my pants, kicking them across the floor. Gus tucks his fingers beneath the elastic of my knickers, tugging them slowly down my thighs with a groan.

He pulls me towards him, and I willingly comply, straddling his thighs. He slides on home as I lower myself over him, and we both let out a low groan.

His hands rest on the small of my back as I begin to rock my hips at a steady pace. I'm too turned on to take it slow. He slides his body lower on the couch, giving my knees more room behind him, and I gain momentum. My fingers clutch at his shoulders, finally clasping around the back of his neck.

I can feel my orgasm building like a tightly coiled spring, ready to let loose, when a sudden jolt of pain erupts in my hip and I lunge sideways. "Ah, shit!" I hiss between my teeth as my leg thrusts out behind me, trying to ease the cramp.

"You okay?" Gus asks, his hips still attempting to move against my now rigid body.

"Cramp," I manage to grit out as my muscle spasms. "I can't..." I pull off him, lying prone on the couch with my arse in the air. "I need to keep my leg straight."

"You want to stop?" he asks, and the optimistic tone of his voice almost makes me laugh.

"No, we can keep going. Just—" I wiggle my butt side-to-side, "—you'll have to take it from here."

"Are you sure?"

I rest my cheek against my forearm as I shake my butt at him again. "Climb aboard, cowboy."

"You don't have to tell me twice." He climbs out from beneath me and settles himself over the backs of my thighs. "This okay?"

"Mmhmm."

With a little pressure from his palms, he arches my arse higher then in one swift movement, he plunges deep inside. "Fuck," he murmurs.

He pulls almost all the way out before thrusting in to the hilt again and again.

I raise my head a touch, and my fingers grip onto the couch cushion as I try to angle my hips up further. His breaths grow louder with each thrust, and I know he's getting close.

I tilt further still, and that's when it happens.

I take a breath at the wrong time.

As I'm breathing out, he's thrusting in, and I let out a deep, guttural sound in time with his hips as my breath is forced out of me.

He slows, his body angling down towards me. "Are you okay?"

I bury my face in the cushion, nodding. "Mmhmm." And then, to make things worse, I start to laugh. "That was such an unsexy sound," I snort.

He chuckles. "I don't mind."

But my brain keeps playing the sound over and over, and I can't stop laughing.

Gus, God bless him, is still trying to continue, but I'm done for. Every time I stop laughing, it only lasts a few seconds before I hear it again and start up again.

"Stop laughing, you're pushing me out!" Gus cries, still desperately trying to finish what we started.

This does not have the desired effect he was hoping for. I laugh so hard that I feel him slip out altogether.

He sighs, rolling off me and landing on the floor, his head falling onto my back.

"I'm sorry," I manage to say between bursts, but it's like I'm a child again and can't control myself.

Gus picks up my knickers, holding them aloft on one finger. "I've changed my mind. I don't think these are very lucky at all."

Chapter eighteen

I didn't wear my lucky knickers again over our honeymoon, cautious not to have a repeat of that fateful day, and the rest of our time seemed to fly by without issue. On our final day in Hanmer, we packed our bags and said our goodbyes to our little bungalow of love, promising to return again one day.

"I'm going to miss this place," I say wistfully as we pull out of the driveway for the last time. We stop at the end of our road, at the intersection leading to the walkway up the hill. "I'm not going to miss that though." I flip the hill the bird as Gus pulls out onto the road and takes us through the village.

"Come on. We had an adventure, didn't we?" He grins, and despite myself, I grin back.

"Yeah, I suppose we did."

The village is only just beginning to wake up, its tourists stepping out into the cool air to grab their early-morning coffees. Vendors mill about the centre of town, setting up for yet another market day. Steam billows out from behind the thermal pool complex, ready for a day of pampering its guests. The trees that line the way in and out of the village sway gently in the breeze, waving their goodbyes as we pass the welcome sign.

"Maybe we should make this a yearly thing. What do you think?" Gus suggests with a relaxed sigh. "We could come back for our anniversary. Recreate our honeymoon." He takes my hand, bringing it to his lips.

"Sounds like a plan, my man. Hell, maybe I could give the old hill another shot." I snort, shaking my head. "Only next time we need to bring food with us and stick to the track." I grab my takeaway cup of coffee and lift it to my lips.

Gus chuckles. "Done." He glances at me before continuing, "But maybe next time, leave the not-so-lucky knickers behind, okay?"

I almost spit my coffee across the window, and another unsexy, unladylike noise escapes me. I clamp my hand over my mouth as I erupt into a fit of laughter. With lightning-quick reflexes, Gus lunges for my cup, removing it from my hands before I can spill it anywhere and placing it into the cup holder between us.

He shakes his head, but his lips curve up into a mischievous grin. "From now on, we make our own luck."

A Note from the Author

Thank you so much for taking the time to read Lady Luck! I was asked to take part in an anthology called Lucky Star, and I decided it was the perfect fit for Susan to get a little bit more airtime, and thus Lady Luck was born. I've even extended it out to give you more of Susan and Gus.

Hopefully you enjoyed reading it as much as I enjoyed writing it. If you did, I would love it if you could leave a review. Reviews not only help our work to be seen, they also offer valuable feedback.

If you would like to keep up to date with my releases, please feel free to sign up to my newsletter. I promise, I won't spam you!

Once again, thank you for reading!

Stacey xxx

Newsletter sign-up: http://eepurl.com/cULu_f

Lady Luck

Acknowledgements

I have to give thanks to the lovely Johanna Rae, who asked me to take part in a charity anthology for the Ages of Pages book signing. Without her, this story never would've come about, but I'm so glad it did. I felt like Suz needed to have a little bit of her own fun.

I'd also like to thank my wonderful husband, without whom I would not know it was possible to get lost while climbing Conical Hill. This actually did happen to us on our honeymoon, and that's what inspired that part of the story (with a few embellishments).

And, of course, to my amazing friend and editor. Trina, you always have my back and make every book fun. Thanks for being on this journey with me.

And finally, to all the readers out there who take a chance on an author giving her all. I appreciate each and every one of you!

Lady Luck

About the Author

Stacey resides in Ashburton, New Zealand with her husband and three children. She is a qualified proofreader, author, wife, mother, and self-proclaimed culinary goddess. When she's not busy writing or editing books, she enjoys reading and procrastinating on TikTok.

She absolutely loves hearing from readers, so please feel free to reach out via email, Instagram, or join her reader group, Broadbent's Bookish Babes.

www.staceybroadbent.com

Other Books by Stacey Broadbent

Hellhounds MC series
Cut Loose
Break Loose
Let Loose (coming soon)

Standalone
Never Judge a Book
Deep Heat
Fever
Emma
Broken

A Step in Time series
Dancing through the Storm
Dancing in Circles
Dancing with Destiny
A Step in Time: the complete series

Super Mum series
Frazzled
Frazzled and Frumpy
Frazzled, Frumpy and Fabulous!
Super Mum: the complete series

Lady Luck

Dark sins novellas
Sins of the Flesh
Mine

Short Stories and Poetry
Musings, Mournings, and Misadventures
Musings, Mayhem, and Mystery
Musings, Magic, and Mischief

Anthologies
Scars to your Beautiful
Witching Hour: Vices and Virtues
The White Ribbon Collection
Key to my Heart
A Touch of Inspiration
No Place Like Home
Serendipity
Lucky Star

Lady Luck

Connect with the Author

www.staceybroadbent.com

www.facebook.com/StaceyBroadbentAuthor

Broadbent's Bookish Babes: https://goo.gl/FY9wQN

www.amazon.com/author/staceybroadbent

Goodreads: https://goo.gl/YJ6dXa

www.instagram.com/authorstaceybroadbent/

www.bookbub.com/authors/stacey-broadbent

www.tiktok.com/@authorstaceybroadbent

www.ingramcontent.com/pod-product-compliance
Lightning Source LLC
Chambersburg PA
CBHW050859130726
47900CB00013B/730